T/O: SYDNEY

FOLLOW YOUR DREAMS!

Jock

Adventures In A Far Away Land

JC Jackman

There's adventure on the horizon, you can feel it in the air. Close your eyes and imagine and I will take you there. To a Far Away Land, where castles still do stand. Where knights are brave and bold and the stories never grow old. It's a wonderful place, time can not erase, it's a dream for all to see. Just close your eyes and make a wish, and then there you'll be . . . In a Far Away Land!

May all your adventures have
happy endings - truly . . .

-JC Jackman

ISBN 978-1-891895-01-2

www.jcjackman.com

Signature Book Printing, Inc.
www.sbpbooks.com
First Printing, April, 2016
Printed in USA

The adventure starts here!

NAME:

AGE:

ADVENTURING FRIEND:
(pick one)

Dragon* Knight in shining armor* Princess*
Elf* Good Monster* Unicorn* Other:

THIS SPELL'S FOR YOU

"Oh…welcome my friends, it's so good to see you! Yes, yes…OK…I will! Zzaps, my dragon welcomes you too.

Now then, my friends, why have you come? No…no…don't tell me! Oh…this is so much fun!

Ah…yes, that's right, of course; this spell's for you.

Look deep into my eyes, yes that's right, now there is much to do.

LIGHT ABRIGHT INTO THIS NIGHT * PREPARE YOURSELF FOR A WONDERFUL SIGHT
JUST A TOUCH OF RAINBOW'S END * A SPLASH OF MOON DUST * OH…AND THEN
A WISHING STAR MADE COMPLETE * AND LET'S NOT FORGET A SPECIAL TREAT
DRAGON'S A SNOOZE ON A MAGICAL BED * WONDERFUL THOUGHTS NOW FILL YOUR HEAD
KAZAM-KRACK ZIP-ZIGGLES
(now this is the best part)
GRUMPH A GAG-A-LING TILL HE GIGGLES
TING-TANG POW ZOWIE…HA HA, JUST FOR YOU
MAY ALL OF YOUR DREAMS SOME DAY COME TRUE!"

DRAGON DREAMS

One of my favorite dreams in the whole wide world is to ride on a dragon!

Can you just imagine what a thrill it would be, to climb on a dragon and truly see, all the fun and adventure that there could be!

I would hold on tight as he prepares for flight, by flapping his huge, powerful wings...what a sight!

Then with a ROAR we'd take to the sky, with tremendous speed, just my dragon and I.

Till we burst through the clouds and there we'd see, an ocean of beauty, white fluffy majesty.

Oh...no roller-coaster could even compare, to the tummy-tickling experience that we'd have there; a dragon sky dive!

Yaaaahooooo.....straight down almost to the ground, then at last, pull up, pull up...Whew!

Swooping and sailing, twisting and turning, seeing as far as the eyes can see going anywhere you want to go, feeling totally free!

Yep, take me to my dragon; it's the only place for me!

The Princess's Dragon

"Come down here at once you overgrown lizard!" the Black Knight commanded that night.

"How am I to prove my love for the Princess if you will not come down and fight!

Now, you sorry excuse for a dragon, come down and taste my steel!

Don't make me climb up to get you or you'll be my breakfast meal!"

"Sir...excuse me...a...Black Knight...Sir," interrupted a blacksmith passing by.

"Do you know what dragon you challenge?" He asked with a sigh.

"Dragon? You call that whimpering worm a dragon? Ha ha!" Laughed the Black Knight.

"Oh please!

I used to eat dragons like him for breakfast. I'll flick him like a flea.

Just wait 'till I get my hands on him; I'll show you what dragon he is! Now please don't you stress."

"Um...Sir...ahem...," the blacksmith said, "that dragon belongs to the Princess!"

GOTCHA!

In a desperate attempt to seek shelter from a terrible storm; Ki-Ti the elf and his dragon friend, Soar, discover a deep dark cave.

To their misfortune it is none other then the cave of Grumph, a mean Grum-Grolac whose cave is a gruesome grave.

For you see, Grumph's priceless treasure is the envy of all the Grum-Grolacs and he is afraid of it being taken.

So when he saw elf and dragon, Grumph's eyes turned red, his face turned blue, he was so mad he was shakin'!

He roared and smashed his fists on the walls and tried to snatch them right out of the air.

Ki-Ti made quickly for the door; they could see the light, they were almost there.

They could smell the rain and feel the wind when...

"HA...HA...HA...ALMOST GOT AWAY THOUGHT-CHA!

WELL...HA...HA...HA...NOW I GOTCHA!"

(to be continued…)

There's A Dragon On My Head!

Do you know what? Don't be alarmed! Please don't be scared. Whatever you do, don't make any sudden moves. For you see, there's a dragon on my head! I don't know where it came from and I really don't care, but he likes my head and he's going to stay there! He sleeps and he snores and he drools green goo. Oh, what in the world do you suppose I should do?
Now, wait just a minute, don't laugh for it's true; the very same thing could happen to you!

Take That!

"Take that!...And this...you wretched beast! How dare you kidnap my princess and spoil our fun feast!

Did you think you had a chance to make her your bride, with me, her brave knight sitting by her side!

Wo...OUCH! That's hot! A bonk on the head ought to cool you down!

One more trick like that and I'll send you straight out of town.

Now, lower your claws and listen to me.

If you're a good little dragon I might let you go free.

There, that's better, now no more trouble you hear!

Come, my sweet princess, there is nothing to fear."

"GRRRRRRRROARRRRR!"

"Ah-ha...pounce at me from behind, now I know you've lost your mind!

I'll just grab you by the tail and swing you round and round!

Then I'll wrap you around a tree and tie you tightly down!

Take that!

Grimgiggles Of Trouble

In a far off kingdom, I don't really know where, there lived three Grimgiggles who
hadn't a care.

Trouble followed them wherever they went, till they came before the King, from whom
they were sent.

"My dear little friends, you must stop and see, all your silly tricks and pranks are
really troubling me.

My people are angry, now listen I say, they all want you out, in a really bad way!"

The Grimgiggles just laughed as they so often do, and pulled each others ears and
their noses, too.

"Enough!" cried the King. "You leave me no choice, to the tower with you!" he said in a
big, booming voice.

So now it's true, right to this day, the Grimgiggles are there, and there they will stay!

Each one bearing reminders to the whole town.

Do nothing but good or truly you'll frown!

The Cave Of No Return

Deep in the forest of Unwanted Dreams, there is a cave of doom, it seems!
I've heard tales of this cave, I know they are true, how someone goes in and then they are through!
No one knows why, no one knows the reason, be it magic or monster or times of the season.
Whatever the reason, I must know why; so you know what, I'll give it a try!
I'll put on my best armor and take up my shield, hold my golden sword high, yes, that's what I'll wield.
Wish me luck, my fine little friend...for who really knows if you'll see me again!

CROSSTANTRUM

Beware the dark mountains of the forbidden pass; a horrible place, if I remember, no trees or grass!

Just cold, hard rock and jagged stones, discarded treasure and dusty bones.

Beware, my friend, or you will surely see; the monster that rules that land across the sea.

Crosstantrum, the dragon, remember his name; his temper and strength are his claim to fame.

He will throw such a fit you never have seen, tear apart mountains and get really mean!

He will scream and shout, throw himself on the ground, breathing hot, raging fire making a terrible sound.

His ear-piercing wailing never seems to end. Oh be careful...be careful...be careful my friend!

May your adventure beat proudly to the sound of the drum, and not to screeches of the terrible Crosstantrum!

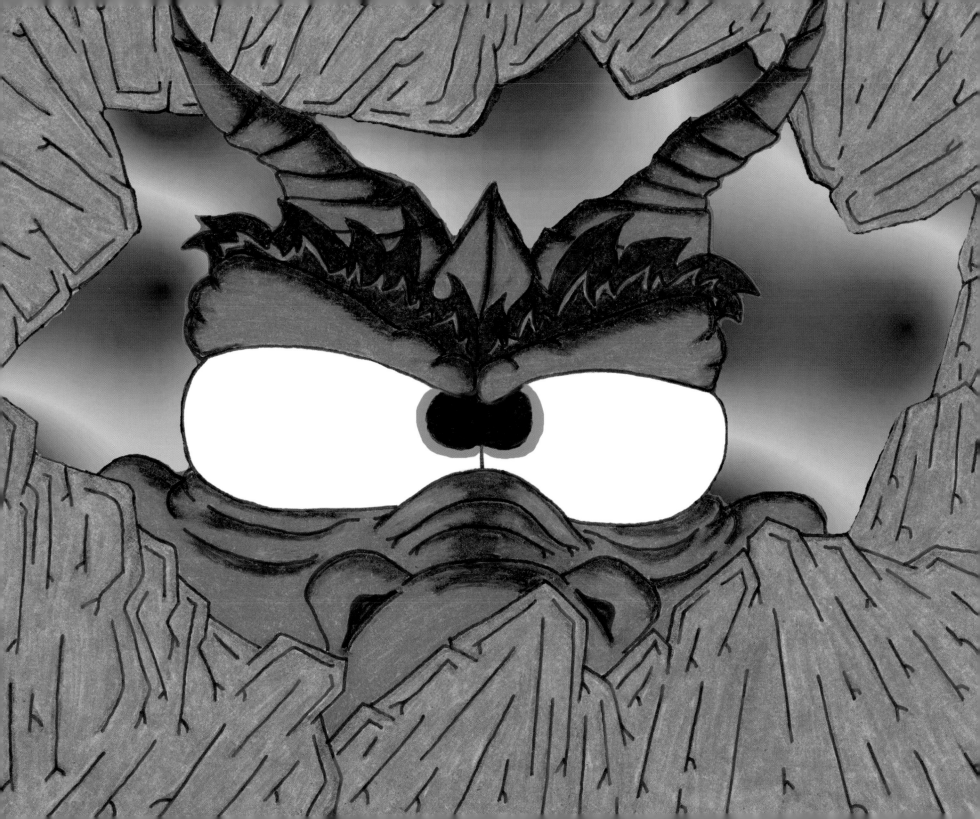

Dreams In The Water

As fast as she could, she ran through the trees, jumping over bushes and rocks with grace-like ease!

What did that slimy little Troll know anyway? He knows nothing of the water so what can he say!

She ran faster still with one thing on her mind, the dreams in the water are they safe? Oh, what would she find?

Down the secret paths she traveled with care. With a great leap down the waterfall, she was there.

The pool of dreams what a wonderful sight! That Troll was just teasing; everything was right.

She looked into the pool with a smile on her face. Dreams sparkled in the water; what a magical place!

Then out of the rocks jumped that mean little Troll! "Ah-ha, now I've found it! Yes, that was my goal!

I tricked you, silly unicorn...you led me straight here. The Dreams in the Water are all mine and I won't share!"

"Well, you clever little Troll, you've found them all right, but how will you get to them? Leap with all your might?"

"What...jump? From way up here?" asked the Troll as he began to fear.

"That's right, it's the only way down." The Troll swallowed hard then started to frown.

"Well... if you can do it; then I can do it, too!"

"I don't think that's a good idea," cried the unicorn. What's the matter with you?"

"Your legs are too short. You will never make it that far!"

"Oh, yeh! Just watch me from right where you are!"

But fall he did, as he tried to leap, from the top of the waterfall, down, down to the deep!

KERRSPLASH!

"Hooray! The Dreams in the Water are safe, yes it's true. They're free from ugly trolls and their craziness too!"

THE GOLDEN SWORD

This hidden treasure at last to claim. Beyond the reaches for Him to gain.
The Dark Knight will never hold this mighty weapon worth more than gold.
With faithful dragon strong and true, Sir James, the knight, knew what to do!

To claim this sword you must be brave, and face many dangers, like the Darkest cave.

To claim this sword you must be kind to everyone and then you'll find, the true power behind this blade is in your heart. Be not afraid.

So, he reached with a steady hand for this Golden Sword to save his land.
Then, with a lot of faith and trust he pulled that sword from out of the dust.

Dunt...dunt...ta...da! The Golden Sword at last is free.
To make the land safe for you and me!

I Love You This Much!

"Daddy...you know what?" the little dragon asked with a smile.
"No, what?" answered his father, listening awhile.
"We really had a fun day...don't you think?"
"Fun day?" said his father giving, him a wink,
"Why, it was the best day of the year!"
"Really?" the little one cried with a cheer.
"You think we can do it again someday?"
"How about tomorrow? What do you say?"
"Well...sure we can!" father said right then and there,
and picked up his dragon and tossed him in the air.
"Weeeeeeee...tee-hee..!" the little dragon giggled and such.
"Daddy...guess what? I love you this much!"

JUST A TREE

Beyond the magic of the Crystal Springs and past the Forest of Unwanted Dreams,
high on a hill looking over the land, is something so special, truly it's grand!
His name is forgotten, far too old some say, but proudly he stands, right to this day!
His treasure is wisdom and many come to see this majestic mark of beauty that some call just a tree.
But if you truly believe and if you stay right there, two big eyes will open up with a smiling face to share.
The most incredible stories you will ever want to hear, of castles, of dragons, of forgotten gold, of lands both far and near,
of pirate ships, and dangerous tasks,
and of silly creatures that live in the grass.
He's stood there for ages, he's seen most everything. Come to him with questions, and answers he will bring.
Yes…of my favorite sights, this is one that you must see, not of castles or of magic treasures, but on a hill, He's just a tree!

About the Author

Be it on stage at the Denver Center of the Performing Arts, on the radio as a local personality with Radio Disney, or visiting bookstores and schools with one of his children's books -his love for adventure, fun and excitement, truly captures the imagination!

WWW.JCJACKMAN.COM

JC lives in Highlands Ranch, Colorado and when he is not writing, drawing or performing, you will find him rock climbing, adventuring, sword fighting or shooting archery with his wife Janae and six kids.

AUTHOR ILLUSTRATOR ACTOR ARTIST MOTIVATIONAL SPEAKER